Charlie
~AND THE~
CHOCOLATE FACTORY™

by ROALD DAHL

An abridged version of the original best-loved story

PUFFIN

PUFFIN BOOKS
Published by the Penguin Group:
London, New York, Ireland, Australia,
Canada, India, New Zealand, and South Africa
Registered Offices: Penguin Books Ltd, 80 Strand,
London WC2R 0RL, England

First published in the United States of America by
Puffin Books, a division of Penguin Young Readers Group, 2005

1 3 5 7 9 10 8 6 4 2

Based on the book *Charlie and the Chocolate Factory*
© Roald Dahl Nominee Ltd, 1964
Photographs and illustrations copyright © Warner Bros.
Entertainment Inc., 2005
Text copyright © Roald Dahl Nominee Ltd, 2005
All rights reserved

ISBN 0-14-240420-9
Printed in the United States of America

This is Charlie.

How d'you do?

And how d'you do?

And how d'you do again?

He is pleased to meet you.

The whole of this family – the six grown-ups and little Charlie Bucket – lived together in a small wooden house on the edge of a great town. There wasn't any question of them being able to buy a better house. They were far too poor for that.

Every one of them – the two old grandfathers, the two old grandmothers, Charlie's father, Charlie's mother and especially little Charlie himself – went about from morning till night with a horrible empty feeling in their tummies.

Charlie felt it worst of all. He desperately wanted something more filling and satisfying than cabbage and cabbage soup. The one thing he longed for more than anything else was . . . CHOCOLATE.

But I haven't yet told you about the one awful thing that tortured little Charlie more than *anything* else. In the town itself, actually within *sight* of the house in which Charlie lived, there was an ENORMOUS CHOCOLATE FACTORY!

And it wasn't simply an ordinary enormous chocolate factory, either. It was the largest and most famous in the whole world! It was WONKA'S FACTORY, owned by a man called Mr Willy Wonka, the greatest inventor and maker of chocolates that there has ever been. And what a tremendous, marvellous place it was!

Twice a day, on his way to and from school, little Charlie Bucket had to walk right past the gates of the factory. And every time he went by, he would begin to walk very, very slowly, and he would hold his nose high in the air and take long deep sniffs of the gorgeous chocolatey smell all around him.

Oh, how he loved that smell!

And oh, how he wished he could go inside the factory and see what it was like!

In the evenings, Charlie always went into the room of his four grandparents to listen to their stories.

"Oh, what a man he is, this Mr Willy Wonka!" cried Grandpa Joe. "Did you know, for example, that he has himself invented more than two hundred kinds of chocolate bars, each with a different centre, each far sweeter and creamier and more delicious than anything the other chocolate factories can make?"

"Perfectly true!" cried Grandma Josephine. "And he sends them to all the four corners of the earth!"

Just then, Mr Bucket, Charlie's father, came into the room. "Have you heard the news?" he cried.

WONKA FACTORY TO BE OPENED
AT LAST TO LUCKY FEW

I, Willy Wonka, have decided to allow five children – just five, mind you, and no more – to visit my factory this year. These lucky five will be shown around personally by me, and then, at the end of the tour, as a special present, all of them will be given enough chocolates and sweets to last them for the rest of their lives! So watch out for the Golden Tickets hidden underneath the wrapping paper of five ordinary bars of chocolate! Good luck to you all, and happy hunting!

(Signed **Willy Wonka**.)

The very next day, the first Golden Ticket was found. The finder was a boy called Augustus Gloop, and Mr Bucket's evening newspaper carried a large picture of him on the front page. The picture showed a nine-year-old who was so enormously fat he looked as though he had been blown up with a powerful pump. Great flabby folds of fat bulged out from every part of his body, and his face was like a monstrous ball of dough with two small greedy curranty eyes peering out upon the world.

"I just *knew* Augustus would find a Golden Ticket," his mother had told the newspapermen. "He eats *so many* bars of chocolate a day that it was almost *impossible* for him *not* to find one. Eating is his hobby, you know."

"What a revolting woman," said Grandma Josephine.

"And what a repulsive boy," said Grandma Georgina.

"Only four Golden Tickets left," said Grandpa George. "I wonder who'll get *those*."

On the day before Charlie Bucket's birthday, the newspapers announced that the second Golden Ticket had been found. The lucky person was a small girl called Veruca Salt who lived with her rich parents.

Mr Salt eagerly explained. "You see, boys, I went out into the town and started buying up all the Wonka bars I could lay my hands on. *Thousands* of them, I must have bought, but three days went by and we had no luck. My little Veruca would lie for hours on the floor, kicking and yelling in the most disturbing way. Now she's all smiles, and we have a happy home once again."

"That's even worse than the fat boy," said Grandma Josephine.

Grandpa Joe said, "No good can ever come from spoiling a child like that, you mark my words."

Only once a year, on his birthday, did Charlie Bucket ever get to taste a bit of chocolate. The whole family saved up their money for that special occasion, and when the great day arrived, Charlie was always presented with one chocolate bar to eat all by himself.

"Happy birthday!" cried the four old grandparents as Charlie came into their room early the next morning.

Charlie smiled nervously. He was holding his present, his only present. WONKA'S WHIPPLE-SCRUMPTIOUS FUDGEMALLOW DELIGHT, it said on the wrapper.

"Just forget about all those Golden Tickets and enjoy the chocolate," Grandpa Joe said.

Then suddenly, as though he couldn't bear the suspense any longer, Charlie tore the wrapper right down the middle. There was no sign of a Golden Ticket anywhere. Charlie looked up. Four kind old faces were watching him intently. He smiled at them, a small sad smile, and then he shrugged his shoulders, picked up the chocolate bar and said, "Here, Mother, have a bit. We'll share it."

And the others all cried, "No, no. It's *all* yours."

That evening, Mr Bucket's newspaper announced,

TWO GOLDEN TICKETS FOUND TODAY.
ONLY ONE MORE LEFT.

"All right," said Grandpa Joe, "let's hear who found them."

"The third ticket," read Mr Bucket, "was found by a Miss Violet Beauregarde."

"'I'm a gum chewer, normally,' she shouted, 'but when I heard about these ticket things of Mr Wonka's, I gave up gum and started on chocolate bars. *Now*, of course, I'm back on gum. I can't do without it.'"

"*Beastly girl*," said Grandma Josephine.

"Despicable!" said Grandma Georgina.

"And who got the fourth Golden Ticket?" Charlie asked.

"Now, let me see," said Mr Bucket. "The fourth Golden Ticket was found by a boy called Mike Teavee. But the lucky winner seemed extremely annoyed by the whole business.

'Can't you fools see I'm watching television?' he said angrily."

"Do *all* children behave like this nowadays?" said Grandma Georgina.

"Now there's only *one ticket left!*" said Grandpa George.

During the next two weeks, the weather turned very cold. After the snow, there came a freezing gale that blew for days and days without stopping. And oh, how bitter cold it was!

The excitement over the Golden Tickets had long since been forgotten. Nobody in the family gave a thought now to anything except the two vital problems of trying to keep warm and trying to get enough to eat.

Then one afternoon, walking back home with the icy wind in his face, Charlie's eye was caught suddenly by something silvery lying in the gutter, in the snow.

It was a fifty-pence piece!

Several people went hurrying past him. Carefully, Charlie pulled it out from under the snow. It meant *one* thing to him at that moment. It meant FOOD.

Automatically, Charlie turned and began moving towards the nearest shop. The man behind the counter looked fat and well-fed. "I think," said Charlie quietly, "I think . . . I'll have one of those chocolate bars."

"Why not?" the shopkeeper said.

Charlie picked it up and tore off the wrapper . . . and *suddenly* . . . from underneath the wrapper . . . there came a brilliant flash of gold.

Charlie's heart stood still.

"It's a Golden Ticket!" screamed the shopkeeper. "I'm awfully glad you got it. Good luck to you, sonny."

"Thank you," Charlie said, and off he went, running through the snow as fast as his legs would go. And five minutes later he arrived at his own home.

"*Mother!*" yelled Charlie, rushing in like a hurricane. "IT'S THE FIFTH GOLDEN TICKET, AND I'VE FOUND IT!"

Grandpa Joe threw up his arms and yelled, "*Yippeeeeeeee!*" And at the same time, in one fantastic leap, this old fellow of ninety-six and a half jumped on to the floor and started doing a dance of victory in his pyjamas.

"Let me see it, Charlie," Mr Bucket said.

"Read it aloud," said Grandpa Joe.

Mr Bucket held the lovely Golden Ticket up close to his eyes. He cleared his throat and said, "All right, I'll read it:

"*Greetings to you*, the lucky finder of this Golden Ticket, from Mr Willy Wonka! I shake you warmly by the hand! Tremendous things are in store for you! Many wonderful surprises await you! In your wildest dreams you could not imagine that such things could happen to you! Just wait and see! The day I have chosen for the visit is the first day in the month of February. You must come to the factory gates at ten o'clock sharp. Don't be late!

(Signed) **Willy Wonka.**"

Mrs Bucket said, "Now, who is going to go with Charlie to the factory?"

"I will!" shouted Grandpa Joe. "I'll look after him! You leave it to me!"

Outside the gates of Wonka's factory, enormous crowds of people had gathered to watch the five lucky ticket holders going in.

Mr Wonka was standing all alone just inside the open gates of the factory.

"Welcome, my little friends! Welcome to the factory!" he called out.

The big fat boy stepped up. "I'm Augustus Gloop," he said.

"Augustus!" cried Mr Wonka "My *dear* boy, how *good* to see you! Delighted! Charmed!"

"My name," said the next child to go forward, "is Veruca Salt."

"My *dear* Veruca! How *do* you do? What a pleasure this is! You *do* have an interesting name, don't you?"

The next two children, Violet Beauregarde and Mike Teavee, came forward. And last of all, a small nervous voice whispered, "Charlie Bucket."

"Charlie!" cried Mr Wonka. "Well, well, well! You're the one who found your ticket only yesterday, aren't you? *Just* in time, my dear boy!"

Charlie glanced back and all sight of the outside world disappeared.

Augustus Gloop

Veruca Salt

Mike Teavee

"Here we are!" cried Mr Wonka. "Through this big red door, please!"

"How lovely and warm!" whispered Charlie.

"I know. And what a marvellous smell!" answered Grandpa Joe.

"Now *this*, my dear children," said Mr Wonka, "this is the main corridor. Follow me!" He trotted off rapidly down the corridor with the tails of his plum-coloured velvet coat flapping behind him, and the visitors all hurried after him. The place was like a gigantic rabbit warren.

Suddenly, Mr Wonka stopped. In front of him there was a shiny metal door. On the door in large letters it said: THE CHOCOLATE ROOM.

Violet Beauregarde

Charlie Bucket

"An important room, this!" cried Mr Wonka. "The heart of the whole business! And so *beautiful*! But do be careful, my dear children! Don't lose your heads!"

They were looking down upon a lovely valley.

"*There!*" cried Mr Wonka, pointing his cane at a great brown river. "It's *all* chocolate! Every drop of that river is hot melted chocolate of the finest quality."

Suddenly, the air was filled with screams of excitement. The screams came from Veruca Salt. "*Look!*" she screamed. "It's a little *person*! It's a little *man*!"

The tiny men – they were no larger than medium-sized dolls – were staring back across the river at the visitors.

"But they can't be *real* people," Charlie said.

"Of course they're real people," Mr Wonka answered. "They're Oompa-Loompas."

Augustus Gloop had sneaked down to the river and was scooping hot melted chocolate into his mouth as fast as he could.

"Augustus!" called out Mrs Gloop. "Come away from that river at once!"

"Augustus," cried Mr Wonka, "you *must* come away. You are dirtying my chocolate!"

Suddenly, there was a shriek, and then a splash, and into the river went Augustus Gloop, and in one second he had disappeared under the brown surface.

"*There he goes!*" somebody shouted, pointing upwards.

Mr Wonka turned around and clicked his fingers sharply. Immediately, an Oompa-Loompa appeared.

"Now listen to me!" said Mr Wonka. "I want you to take Mr and Mrs Gloop up to the Fudge Room and help them to find their son, Augustus. He's just gone up the pipe."

"Off we go!" cried Mr Wonka. "Hurry up, everybody! And please don't worry about Augustus Gloop. He's bound to come out in the wash. They always do."

A steamy mist was rising up now from the great warm chocolate river, and out of the mist there appeared suddenly a most fantastic pink boat.

"This is my private yacht!" cried Mr Wonka, beaming with pleasure. "Isn't she beautiful!"

As soon as everyone was safely in, the Oompa-Loompas pushed the boat away from the bank and began to row. The boat sped on down the river. There was some kind of a dark tunnel ahead. "Row on!" shouted Mr Wonka. "Full speed ahead!" And with the Oompa-Loompas rowing faster than ever, the boat shot into the pitch-dark tunnel.

"Switch on the lights!" shouted Mr Wonka. The river of chocolate was flowing very fast inside the pipe, and the Oompa-Loompas were all rowing like mad. Mr Wonka clapped his hands and laughed and kept glancing at his passengers to see if they were enjoying it as much as he.

But five seconds later, when a bright red door came into sight ahead, he suddenly shouted, "Stop the boat!"

On the door it said,

INVENTING ROOM
PRIVATE – KEEP OUT

Mr Wonka took a key from his pocket, leaned over the side of the boat and put the key in the keyhole.

"*This* is the most important room in the entire factory!" he said. "All my most secret new inventions are cooking and simmering in here! No touching, no meddling and no tasting!"

Charlie Bucket stared. The whole place was filled with smoke and steam and delicious rich smells.

Mr Wonka led the party over to a gigantic machine. "Here we go!" he cried, and he pressed three different buttons on the side of it. Then suddenly, the machine let out a monstrous mighty groan and a tiny drawer popped out. In it lay something so small and thin and grey that everyone thought it must be a mistake.

"You mean that's *all*?"
said Mike Teavee, disgusted.
There was a pause. Then suddenly,
Violet Beauregarde let out a yell of excitement.
"By gum, it's *gum!*" she shrieked. "It's a stick
of chewing-gum!"
"Right you are!" cried Mr Wonka. "It's a
stick of the most *amazing* and *fabulous*
and *sensational* gum in the world!"

"This gum," Mr Wonka went on, "is my latest, my greatest, my most fascinating invention! That tiny little strip lying there is a whole three-course dinner all by itself!"

"What *do* you mean? It's tomato soup, roast beef and blueberry pie?" said Violet Beauregarde. "Hand over this magic gum of yours and we'll see if the thing works."

"I would rather you didn't take it," Mr Wonka told her gently. "You see, I haven't got it *quite right* yet."

Suddenly, before Mr Wonka
could stop her, she shot out her hand
and grabbed the stick of gum and popped it into
her mouth.

Little Charlie Bucket was staring at her absolutely
spellbound. Her face and hands and legs and neck turned
a brilliant purplish-blue, the colour of blueberry juice!

"I feel most peculiar," gasped Violet.

"Great heavens, girl!" screeched Mrs Beauregarde.

"You're blowing up like a balloon!"

"Like a blueberry," said Mr Wonka.

There was no saving her now.

"It *always* happens like
that ," sighed Mr Wonka. "It's
most annoying."

Mr Wonka clicked his fingers,
and ten Oompa-Loompas appeared.

"Take her along to the Juicing Room
at once. We've got to squeeze the
juice out of her immediately."

"Well, well, well," sighed Mr Willy Wonka, "two naughty little children gone. Three good little children left. I think we'd better get out of this room quickly before we lose anyone else!"

Charlie Bucket saw that they were now back in one of those long pink corridors with many other pink corridors leading out of it. Mr Wonka was rushing along in front, turning left and right and right and left, and Grandpa Joe was saying, "Keep a good hold of my hand, Charlie. It would be terrible to get lost in here."

They passed a door in the wall. "No time to go in!" shouted Mr Wonka. "Press on! Press on!"

Mr Wonka rushed on down the corridor.

THE NUT ROOM, it said on the next door they came to.

"All right," said Mr Wonka, "stop here for a moment and take a peek. But don't go in! Whatever you do, don't go into THE NUT ROOM!"

It was an amazing sight. One hundred squirrels were seated upon high stools. There were mounds and mounds of walnuts, and the squirrels were all working away like mad, shelling the walnuts at speed.

"Hey, Mummy!" shouted Veruca Salt suddenly. "Get me one of those squirrels! I want one."

"They're not for sale," Mr Wonka answered. "She can't have one."

"Who says I can't!" shouted Veruca. "I'm going in."

"Don't!" said Mr Wonka, but he was too late. The girl had already thrown open the door.

"All right," Veruca said. "I'll have *you!*"

She reached out her hands to grab a pretty little squirrel and every single squirrel around the table took a flying leap towards her. One climbed up on to her shoulder and started tap-tap-tapping the wretched girl's head.

"They're testing her to see if she's a bad nut," said Mr Wonka.

Then all at once, the squirrels pulled Veruca to the ground and started carrying her across the floor.

"By golly, she *is* going down the chute!" said Mr Salt.

"Then save her!" cried Mrs Salt.

"Too late," said Mr Wonka. "That *particular* chute runs directly into the great big main rubbish pipe which carries away all the rubbish from every part of the factory."

Both Mr and Mrs Salt dashed into the Nut Room and ran over to the hole in the floor.

"Veruca!" shouted Mrs Salt. "Are you down there?" She needed only one tiny little push . . . and *that* is exactly what the squirrels gave her!

"Good gracious me!" said Mr Salt.

The squirrels rushed up behind him . . .

"Help!" he shouted.

But he was already toppling forward, and down the chute he went, just as his wife had done before him – and his daughter.

"I've never seen anything like it!" cried
Mr Wonka. "The children are disappearing
like rabbits. But they'll *all* come out in the wash."
He skipped across the passage to a pair of
double doors. The doors slid open.
        "Now then," cried Mr Wonka,
        "which button shall we press first?
Take your pick!"
Charlie Bucket stared around him in astonishment.
"This isn't just an ordinary up-and-down lift!"
announced Mr Wonka proudly. "This lift can go
sideways and longways and slantways and any other
way you can think of!"
        Quickly, Charlie started reading the labels alongside
the buttons.

THE ROCK-CANDY MINE – 10,000 FEET DEEP,

it said on one.

Then ... STRAWBERRY-JUICE WATER PISTOLS.

STICKJAW FOR TALKATIVE PARENTS.

"Isn't there a *Television Room* in all this lot?" asked
Mike Teavee.

"Certainly," Mr Wonka said. "That button over there."

"*Whoopee!*" shouted Mike Teavee. "That's for me!"
Instantly, there was a tremendous whizzing noise. The
doors clanged shut and the lift leaped away. But it
leaped sideways!

The next moment, there was a screaming of brakes, and
the lift began to slow down. Then it stopped altogether.

Mr Wonka said, "Just a minute now! Listen to me! I want everybody to be very careful in this room. There is dangerous stuff around in here and you *must not* tamper with it."

The Teavee family, together with Charlie and Grandpa Joe, stepped out of the lift into a room so bright and dazzlingly white that they screwed up their eyes in pain.

There was an enormous camera on wheels, and a whole army of Oompa-Loompas.

"Here we go!" cried Mr Wonka. "This is the Testing Room for my very latest and greatest invention – Television Chocolate! I shall now send a bar of my very best chocolate from one end of this room to the other – by television!"

One of the Oompa-Loompas caught hold of a large switch and pulled it down.

"The chocolate's gone!" shouted Grandpa Joe.

Suddenly, a small bar of chocolate appeared in the middle of the screen.

"Take it!" shouted Mr Wonka.

Charlie put out his hand and touched the screen, and the bar of chocolate came away in his fingers.

"Eat it!" shouted Mr Wonka. "It'll be delicious! It's the same bar! It's got smaller on the journey, that's all!"

"What about people?" asked Mike Teavee.

"A person!" cried Mr Wonka. "Are you off your rocker?"

"But could it be done?"

"Good heavens, child, I really don't know ... I suppose it *could* ..."

Mike Teavee was already off and running. "Look at me!" he shouted. "I'm going to be the first person in the world to be sent by television!"

"*No, no, no, no!*" cried Mr Wonka.

But there was no stopping Mike Teavee. The crazy boy rushed on, and when he reached the enormous camera, he jumped straight for the switch, scattering Oompa-Loompas right and left. As he did so, he leaped out into the full glare of the mighty lens.

There was a blinding flash.

A tiny little voice, no louder than the squeaking of a mouse, came out of the television set. "Hi, Pop! Look at *me*!" He was not more than an inch tall.

"He's *shrunk*!" said Mr Teavee.

"Of course he's shrunk," said Mr Wonka. "What did you expect?"

"This is terrible!" wailed Mrs Teavee. "What *are* we going to do?"

"Well," said Mr Wonka, "we'll put him in a special machine for testing the stretchiness of chewing-gum."

He clicked his fingers. An Oompa-Loompa appeared immediately. "Follow these orders," said Mr Wonka, handing the Oompa-Loompa a piece of paper. "You'll find the boy in his father's pocket."

"Which room shall it be next?" said Mr Wonka as he darted into the lift. "And how many children are there left now?"

Little Charlie looked at Grandpa Joe, and Grandpa Joe looked back at little Charlie.

"But, Mr Wonka," Grandpa Joe called after him, "there's only Charlie left now."

Mr Wonka swung round and stared at Charlie. There was a silence.

"You mean you're the *only* one left?" he said, pretending to be surprised.

"Why, yes," whispered Charlie. "Yes."

"But, my *dear boy*," he cried out, "*that means you've won!* Well *done*, Charlie, well *done*! Now the fun is really going to start! But we mustn't dilly. We mustn't dally! Luckily for us, we have the great glass lift to speed things up!"

Mr Wonka was reaching for a button high up on the glass ceiling of the lift. It said . . . UP AND OUT.

"Up and *out*," thought Charlie. "What sort of a room is that?"

WHAM! The lift shot straight up like a rocket!

Then suddenly, *CRASH!* Grandpa Joe shouted, "Help! We're done for!" and Mr Wonka said, "No, we're not! We're through! We're out!"

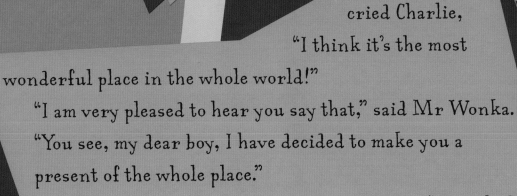

The great glass lift was now
hovering high over the town.
"How I love my chocolate factory,"
said Mr Wonka, gazing down.
"Do you love it too, Charlie?"
he asked.

"Oh, yes,"
cried Charlie,
"I think it's the most
wonderful place in the whole world!"

"I am very pleased to hear you say that," said Mr Wonka.
"You see, my dear boy, I have decided to make you a
present of the whole place."

"*Giving* it to him?" gasped Grandpa Joe. "But why?"

"I've got no family at all," Mr Wonka said. "So who
is going to run the factory when I get too old to do it
myself? *Someone's* got to keep it going."

"*So that* is why you sent out the Golden Tickets!"
cried Charlie.

"Exactly!" said Mr Wonka. "We must go and fetch
the rest of the family," he cried. He pressed some buttons
and the lift shot downwards towards Charlie's house.

CRASH!

went the lift, right through
the roof into the old people's bedroom.

"Save us!" cried Grandma Josephine.

"Mother!" cried Charlie. "We're all going to live in
Mr Wonka's factory and he's given it *all* to me."

It took quite a time for Grandpa Joe and Charlie to
explain to everyone what had been happening to them.

Charlie climbed on to the bed. "Please don't be
frightened," he said. "We're going to the most
wonderful place in the world!"

"Charlie's right," said Grandpa Joe.

"Will there be anything to eat when we get
there?" asked Grandma Josephine.

"Anything to *eat*?" cried Charlie, laughing.

"Oh, you just wait and see!"